Dear Parent:
Your child's love of reading starts here!

Every child learns to read in a different way and at his or her own speed. Some go back and forth between reading levels and read favorite books again and again. Others read ~~through each level in~~ order. You can help your young reader impr ~~ove and grow more~~ confident by encouraging his or her own int ~~erests and abilities. From~~ books your child reads with you to the first ~~books he or she reads~~ alone, there are I Can Read Books for every ~~stage of reading:~~

SHARED READING
Basic language, word repetition, and whimsical illustrations, ideal for sharing with your emergent reader

BEGINNING READING
Short sentences, familiar words, and simple concepts for children eager to read on their own

READING WITH HELP
Engaging stories, longer sentences, and language play for developing readers

READING ALONE
Complex plots, challenging vocabulary, and high-interest topics for the independent reader

I Can Read Books have introduced children to the joy of reading since 1957. Featuring award-winning authors and illustrators and a fabulous cast of beloved characters, I Can Read Books set the standard for beginning readers.

A lifetime of discovery begins with the magical words "I Can Read!"

Visit www.icanread.com for information
on enriching your child's reading experience.

I Can Read® and I Can Read Book® are trademarks of HarperCollins Publishers.

Spies in Disguise: Meet the Spies
Spies in Disguise™ & © 2019 Twentieth Century Fox Film Corporation.
All rights reserved. Printed in the United States of America.
No part of this book may be used or reproduced in any manner whatsoever without written permission except
in the case of brief quotations embodied in critical articles and reviews. For information address HarperCollins
Children's Books, a division of HarperCollins Publishers, 195 Broadway, New York, NY 10007.

ISBN 978-0-06-285296-0

19 20 21 22 23   LSCC   10 9 8 7 6 5 4 3 2 1   ❖   First Edition

I Can Read!

1 BEGINNING READING

Blue Sky STUDIOS

SPIES IN DISGUISE

MEET THE SPIES

Adapted by Alexandra West

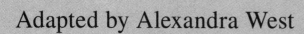

HARPER
An Imprint of HarperCollinsPublishers

This is Lance Sterling.

He is a spy.

Doesn't he look like a spy?

He wears a suit and a bow tie.

Lance travels in style.

He drives a fast car.

Lance drank a formula.

It turned him into a bird!

Birds do not look like spies.

This is Walter Beckett.

He gave Lance the formula.

Walter wants to help save the world.

To save the world,

Walter will need to help Lance.

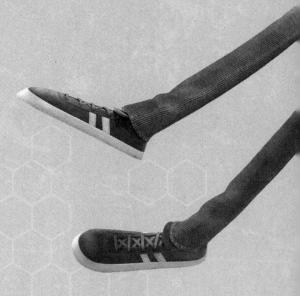

This is Joyless.

Joyless runs the spy agency.

She cares about Lance.

Marcy is an agent.

It is her job to track down anyone

who breaks the rules.

She thinks Lance broke the rules.

This is Eyes.

She works for Marcy.

Eyes can see everything!

She uses her super glasses.

This is Ears.

He also works for Marcy.

Ears can hear everything!

He uses his audio dish.

This is Killian.

He has a robot arm.

Killian made everyone

think that Lance is bad.

Lance has to prove that he's a good guy.

He needs to find Killian!

But Lance is just a tiny bird.

A bird named Lovey wants to help!

Lovey loves Lance.
But Lance does not
love Lovey.

25

Jeff joins Lovey and Lance.

He comes in handy

because he is big.

Crazy Eyes also joins the team.

He is very hungry.

He ate a gadget

and now he can spit fire!

This is Lance's new team.

They don't look or act like spies.

But together they can

save the world.

The world is full of spies.

Together they can save the world.